Essex Authors

Edited By Debbie Killingworth

First published in Great Britain in 2018 by:

 YoungWriters

Young Writers
Remus House
Coltsfoot Drive
Peterborough
PE2 9BF
Telephone: 01733 890066
Website: www.youngwriters.co.uk

FOREWORD

Young Writers was created in 1991 with the express purpose of promoting and encouraging creative writing. Each competition we create is tailored to the relevant age group, hopefully giving each child the inspiration and incentive to create their own piece of work, whether it's a poem or a short story. We truly believe that seeing their work in print gives pupils a sense of achievement and pride in their work and themselves.

Every day children bring their toys to life, creating fantastic worlds and exciting adventures, using nothing more than the power of their imagination. What better subject then for primary school pupils to write about, capturing these ideas in a mini saga – a story of just 100 words. With so few words to work with, these young writers have really had to consider their words carefully, honing their writing skills so that every word counts towards creating a complete story.

Within these pages you will find stories about toys coming to life when we're not looking, the adventures they have with their owners and even a few tales of peril when toys go missing or get lost! Each one showcases the creativity and talent of these budding new writers as they learn the skills of writing, and we hope you are as entertained by them as we are.

CONTENTS

Independent Entries

Oscar George Phillips (10)   1
Lewis Brimfield   2

Cooks Spinney Academy & Nursery, Cooks Spinney

Yu-Yao Wang (8)   3
Guilherme Fialho (9)   4
Jasmine Wright (9)   5
Violet Cogan (10)   6
Jess Pope (10)   7
Ayaan Ali (10)   8

Harris Primary Academy Chafford Hundred, Chafford Hundred

Jasleen Lotta (10)   9
Sofia Hudd (10)   10
Emily Grace Eden (10)   11
Daniil Drozdov (10)   12
Oluwatobi Olasehinde-Williams (10)   13
Shazil Erfan (11)   14
Eileen Joseph (11)   15
Mariyah Amira Malik (10)   16
Ameer Abdur Rahman (10)   17
David Abraham (11)   18
Lucy Maragh (10)   19
O'Jani Christopher (10)   20
Robyn Bailey (11)   21
Benjamin Rumsby (11)   22
Alexi Laken Choppy-Godfrey (10)   23
Sophie Hilliard (11)   24
Mia Kaur (11)   25

Tatyanna Daisi (10)   26
Ethan Paul Ridpath (10)   27
Zoya Ariana Irshad (10)   28
Isabelle Durant (11)   29
Lana Ayeni (10)   30
Catherine Tse (11)   31
Leah Gredley (9)   32
Olaoluwani Ademuyiwa (11)   33
Phoebe Sinacola-Webb (10)   34
Ayobami Oye (10)   35
Denisia John (11)   36
Caitlin Emma-Jo Francis (10)   37
Chloe Harrison (9)   38
Rinnah Larbi (10)   39
Tayla Shevket (10)   40
Jamie-Leigh Christine Martin (11)   41
Fiona Ng (11)   42
David Gaitan (10)   43
Charlie O'Rourke (10)   44
Isabella Gui Susan Rice (9)   45
Carmen May Jones (10)   46
George Sinkins (10)   47
Jahziah Blackford (10)   48
Jamie Broom (10)   49
Evan Williams (11)   50
David Nnamchi (10)   51
Maria Horsley (9)   52
James Daniel Cooper (10)   53
Olivia Rose Collard (10)   54
Kelly Ototobor (9)   55
Elizabeth John (9)   56
Holly Clark (9)   57
Billy Dopson (9)   58
Jack Ng (10)   59
Sophie Darrell-Lambert (10)   60

Nana Nyame (10)   61
Sophia Peck (10)   62
Kevindran Indradas (10)   63
Jacob Brown (9)   64
Naima Muchopa (10)   65

Kingswode Hoe School, Colchester

Cadan Robbins (12)   66
Tanya Leonie Norton (12)   67
Ellie-May Taylor (12)   68
Charlie Evans (12)   69
Leanne Wallace (12)   70
Kian Mills (12)   71
Leo Parsons (11)   72
Alex Ruske (11)   73
Lily Eastwood-Bringhurst (11)   74
Katelynn Isabella Dixon (11)   75
Kelly Marshall (11)   76
Jay Bass (12)   77

St Pius X RC Primary School, Chelmsford

Ellie Troy-Pryde   78
Alanna Ella McDonagh (11)   79
Maia Dines (10)   80
Liethuna Kirikaran (11)   81
Robert Crawley (10)   82

The R J Mitchell Primary School, Hornchurch

Kien Tran (8)   83
Chloe Galbraith (8)   84
Jasmine Hall (9)   85
Daniel Erasmus (8)   86
Lily Cain (9)   87
Nicole Martine (8)   88
Harrison Cotton (9)   89
Ara Kayode (8)   90
Bobby Alan Wakeling (9)   91

Wells Primary School, Barclay Oval

Caleb Mills (9)   92
Sophia Tse (9)   93
Benjamin Samuel Bennett (9)   94
Austin MacDonald (9)   95
Lani Oshungbure (9)   96
Lynden Kyte (9)   97
Emily Flora Bell (9)   98
Viktor Zaykov (9)   99
Sahib Panjrath (9)   100
Millie Ryan-Martin (7)   101
Amar Johal (8)   102
Sofiina Jones (9)   103
Reggie Oliver-Simmons (8)   104
Bella Hall (7)   105
Yoanna Peteva (9)   106
Kayra Demir (9)   107
Kyra Mubashar (7)   108
Adeeba Khandokar (9)   109
Mirabelle Rose Morgan (9)   110

THE MINI SAGAS

Star Wars: Rebels Vs Imperial Army

"Men, he's gone, time to ambush the Imperial army!" shouted the Rebel commander to his squad.

Quietly but quickly, they crawled across the carpet to the Imperial's base.

Meanwhile, at the Imperial base, a watch guard spotted a Rebel crawling towards him.

"Ready your guns and prepare for battle!" he cried. "The Rebels are here."

Bam! The rebels realised they had been spotted and started firing. They received shots from the Imperials and...

Footsteps coming up the stairs. Everybody froze and dropped to the ground.

Oscar walked in and thought, *I'm sure I've already put my Lego away...*

Oscar George Phillips (10)

He Lost His House?

Playboot Boon had lost his house. He'd been walking quickly, playing basketball with his eyes. He thought he could see his home. He walked there and it was a big block of brown rock. He was upset.
Then, he found some people and he asked them, "Do you know where I live?"
They replied, "Yes I do."
The people led him to his house and he went into his house at 5am. He got there and went into his kitchen, he touched stinky, old cheese and rotten, red, blue and brown crisps.
"Doh!" he cried. "I cannot believe I'm here."

Lewis Brimfield

Looking For A Friend

There once lived a lonely unicorn on an enchanted island, it wanted a friend.

It asked everyone, "Can I be your friend?"

They said, "No!"

So the unicorn searched for a friend. It looked under rocks, up in trees, underground until the unicorn found a cave. It looked inside and heard a scratching noise!

The unicorn went deeper and deeper until the scratching noise stopped!

The unicorn found a puppy, it asked the unicorn, "Can I be your friend?"

The unicorn said, Yes!" and they lived together happily in the cave, and they had lots of adventures together.

Yu-Yao Wang (8)

Cooks Spinney Academy & Nursery, Cooks Spinney

The Greatest Battle Of Toys

One day, a few toy soldiers decided to invade their neighbour's house and started a war.

So ten minutes later, they started a battle.

Soldier One said, "I've been shot in the head!"

"You don't have a head!" said Soldier Three.

The war was long, it lasted ten minutes. The toys that went to invade had won. It was a defeat for the others. From that day on, there were no more battles and they lived happily ever after. The wars turned into big parties of friendship, full of fun, games and sports and they all became really good friends.

Guilherme Fialho (9)

Cooks Spinney Academy & Nursery, Cooks Spinney

The Magic Toyshop

Once there was a girl called Lacy. She went to a toyshop because that was her job. When Lacy was just closing the shop, a toy moved. All of them moved. A teddy explained about the moving toy bit. Not all toys were good, some were bad. Suddenly, a snake came off the shelves. She got Captain America's shield, then a lightsaber and killed the toy snake.

Lacy told the toys, "Now go back to your shelves but not you, teddy bear, I want to buy you!"

So now all the toys were safe and Lacy had a talking teddy.

Jasmine Wright (9)
Cooks Spinney Academy & Nursery, Cooks Spinney

Phoebe's Toyshop Adventure

Hi, I'm Phoebe and I'm an Our Generation doll and I'm going on a trip to Smyths. I'm going to live there but this place is a store and little kids pick you, buy you and it seems fun. I just hope I make some friends. Did you know you can have a pet? I'm very excited. Oh, yay, we're here! Oh, I'm going to my section.

Two hours later... I've just met this girl called April. She's really nice and kind. No wait, my friend, April has been sold! I'm here with none of my friends, nooo!

Violet Cogan (10)

Cooks Spinney Academy & Nursery, Cooks Spinney

My Bear, Ella

My bear, Ella, walked over to me as I awoke. I sadly noticed a button eye missing. *Oh no*, I thought. It was then I realised, we must find it. Together, we strolled to the kitchen to start the search. Nothing was found. Lounge. Behind the TV? No! Under the sofa? No! Family room? Yes! Upon the desk lie a blue button eye! After sewing it back on, I wondered if it had ever actually fallen off! Ella once again had two blue eyes. Yay! Hooray! Yippee!
"You are the best owner ever!" my toy told me.

Jess Pope (10)
Cooks Spinney Academy & Nursery, Cooks Spinney

Untitled

There was a cute, little boy called Amellio who was playing with his small car. All of his cars came to life and drove out of his door, they were so evil. Then, smart Amellio went to the police station and told them everything that had happened. But the police did nothing.

After a while, Smyths Toys Superstores was there to save the world. Smyths Toys Superstores' boss had an idea. The boss went to the cars, took out their batteries and saved the universe.

Ayaan Ali (10)
Cooks Spinney Academy & Nursery, Cooks Spinney

The Clumsy Bear

Boom, bash, click!
"Dad, be careful!" *Boom, boom, boom!*
A large, hair-raising creature approached the bears.
"Dad, help!" Freddie cried.
"Don't move!"
The creature approached and questioned, "What are these useless things doing here?"
He ignorantly threw them across the room.
"Josh, come here," his mother pleaded.
"Coming," he answered.
Bam! The door slammed shut.
"Phew, he's gone!"
"Wait, what's that?"
"I'm not sure, let's test it."
"Freddie, don't."
However, it was too late, *kaboosh!* Josh's school project of a volcano exploded.
"It's everywhere, what do we do now?"
"Use this useless paint!"
"Hide!" Josh came. "Where is the paint?"

Jasleen Lotta (10)

Harris Primary Academy Chafford Hundred, Chafford Hundred

Christmas Tragedy!

It was Christmas. Santa and his reindeer had all the presents packed for all the children. But as he flew off, Tinkerbell, Unikitty and a fashion Barbie fell out! A horrible tragedy on Christmas Day.

"Ouch!"

"Argh!"

"Ooof!"

"Wait, wait, wait-t-t!" Unikitty cried.

"Great, what are we gonna do now? I must get to Tiffany!" shrieked Barbie.

"So must we!" cried Unikitty and Tinkerbell.

Suddenly, Dasher came out of the shadows.

"Need a ride? They left me too!"

"Yes please!" shouted the lost toys.

Whoosh! They took to the skies!

"We're here! Tiffany's bedroom!"

"Thanks and merry Christmas, everyone!"

Sofia Hudd (10)

Harris Primary Academy Chafford Hundred, Chafford Hundred

The Secret Life Of Pets

As the sky turned black, it was Kate's bedtime.

"Goodnight Kate," whispered her parents as she drifted off to sleep.

"Come, quick!" Barry the bear whispered.

Thud! The dinosaur's tail crashed on a box.

"Aww! I'm such a clumsy-saurus," she exclaimed.

"Huh?" she moaned.

"What's wrong?" her parents asked.

"Nothing," was the answer, and she glared at each toy, especially Destiny Dinosaur.

"Alright..." they said, not fully believing her.

She laid in her bed. Awake. Listening.

"For a punishment, you cannot see Kate for a week," said Gary Gnome.

"No!" said Kate. "I love you all the same!"

Emily Grace Eden (10)

Harris Primary Academy Chafford Hundred, Chafford Hundred

The Away Play

"I'm bored," Player Thirty-Six exclaimed in the night, "I wanna play away."

"Let's play on another pitch!" said the goalkeeper.

"Okay," the team accepted.

So they jumped off the football table and walked.

"So, who are we playing?" said Twenty-One.

"Some random people!" said Fifty-Six.

They continued slowly, walking down to the hole near the heater.

"So boys, we're going through there near the door and heater!" said Captain One.

"We will score some in, ey!" said Thirty-Six.

However, as soon as they reached it, *bang!* The door opened! It was their owner, their manager ruined them all!

Daniil Drozdov (10)

Harris Primary Academy Chafford Hundred, Chafford Hundred

Plushie Squad

"He's gone," said Salmon.

"I'll fly out," said Falcon, finding it impossible to fly.

"We have to get home properly," said Rattlesnake.

"Oh, I have an idea, Turtle, I'll catapult you out of the window," said Cheetah.

"Okay, ouch!" said Turtle.

"I'll glide out," said Draco Lizard.

"You can't," said Panda.

Draco still did and fell to the floor.

"See?" said Panda.

"Incoming baby!" said Turtle.

"But I cannot move," said Salmon.

The baby drooled on Salmon's fish bowl.

"Come on, and the worst part is I'm a real salmon."

Oluwatobi Olasehinde-Williams (10)

Harris Primary Academy Chafford Hundred, Chafford Hundred

The Unfinished Clean-Up

The door opened and Sam walked out of the room.
"The coast is clear!" said the general.
They all walked out calmly.
"Look at me!" cried the bear, but then the blood-red paint fell across the wooden floor.
"Oops!" the fluffy bear exclaimed.
"Clean up team!" ordered the sergeant.
Ten army trucks raced to the site and set up cones and cleared the area.
"Broom away!"
They brushed the area thoroughly with Dettol.
"Get the crane and paint mixer here immediately!" they all said.
They lifted the paint tin and filled it again.
"Go back to your places! He's coming!"

Shazil Erfan (11)

Harris Primary Academy Chafford Hundred, Chafford Hundred

Donation Dance Battle

Creak! Ellie's mum walked in.

"Hey Ellie, you need to donate one of your toys!"
Ellie's mum was digging through Ellie's transparent toy chest.

"Umm Mum, I can't. I love them!"

Ellie's mum shrugged and strode out of Ellie's bedroom, closing the door silently. Ellie smelt the sweet scent of cookies so she followed her mum.

"Nooo!" Barbie shrieked.

"There's only one thing for it... Dance battle!" Ballet Girl yelled.

Stuffed Dragon and Piggy Bank were the least loved toys so they danced. The music played. The toys pranced. The toys leapt. Finally, the battle ended. It was... a tie.

Eileen Joseph (11)

Harris Primary Academy Chafford Hundred, Chafford Hundred

The Puzzle Disaster!

Smash! The colossal box of puzzles dropped onto the cream carpet.

"Sorry!" shouted Clumsy.

"Oh, Clumsy!" cried Woody.

"What are we going to do?" whispered Rex. "Annie is going to come back any minute now!"

"Never fear, Hamm is here!"

"What is your idea then?" bellowed Rex.

"Well, my idea is to find all the pieces as quickly as we can and put them all in the box," replied Hamm.

"Okay, let's get to work," cried Woody.

They all rapidly tried to find all the pieces and put them in the box.

"Quick, get in your box, Annie is home!"

Mariyah Amira Malik (10)

Harris Primary Academy Chafford Hundred, Chafford Hundred

The Midnight Hour

Moonlight slit inside. All sound was dead, apart from the hollow snore. *Bang!* chimed Big Ben. They awoke. Breathing relentlessly. *Vroom! They* sped off hastily, past obstacles.

"Commando," he spoke, before twitching his khaki green uniform.

The car came to a halt. An echo of bullets hammered past. He spotted the enemy. Both were mass flocks of soldiers. Smoke emerged. The German's were on trains. The carpet, which was no-man's-land, was sprayed with bullets. The British flew in planes, parachuting off. The luminous light flicked on. The soldiers lay still. Yet again, midnight was so silent.

"What's that?"

Ameer Abdur Rahman (10)

Harris Primary Academy Chafford Hundred, Chafford Hundred

Young Writers logo

The Chosen Toy

"I wonder who will get picked, hopefully me!" said the pristine robot.

"Definitely not that new toy!" said the pearlescent pony pointing at the slimy dragon.

He said, "Hi, I am so happy to be here."

"Urgh, how disgusting," Pony whispered to Robot.

"Oh, here comes a customer, get ready!" the robot announced.

The customer inspected all the toys carefully, he looked at the dragon and then laughed, saying, "Who would buy this?"

The dragon frowned and others laughed.

Later, a girl came in and immediately grabbed the dragon who then knew that there was a toy for everyone.

David Abraham (11)

Harris Primary Academy Chafford Hundred, Chafford Hundred

The Unforgotten Robot

Darkness cloaked the desolate streets while the substandard plan was plotted by Soldier Two.

"Now we are going to continue to make Tom's life grave!"

Eyes widened and were glued on Soldier Two.

Voices crowded the room, eager for it to go as planned.

"All, we are shipping him to the floods!"

Voices gasped in sheer disbelief.

"Tom will be transported to the toilet! Also known as the unforgotten deep, dark depths of toy horror!"

Gathered together in a huddle, the soldiers hauled Tom into a zone of appalling water - the toilet.

"Adios, amigo!" Soldier Two boasted mercilessly.

Lucy Maragh (10)

Harris Primary Academy Chafford Hundred, Chafford Hundred

The Great Battle

Out of nowhere, a soldier said, "Everyone advance! The enemy is surely in their base. I can smell them!"

They all moved forward, not knowing their enemy was behind them.

"Stay out of sight everyone and make sure you don't lose them!"

The enemy commander said, "Keep moving, everyone, they're bound to be here!"

A gigantic soldier appeared. They ran but they were blocked off by their enemy. They were terrified.

The commander said with a fright on his face, "You can have them!"

The enemy commander said, "What a great commander!"

Suddenly, a shadow appeared...

O'Jani Christopher (10)

Harris Primary Academy Chafford Hundred, Chafford Hundred

The Great Escape

Swoosh! Whoosh! The brave soldiers began to evacuate their base and tiptoed over to the lobby. "On my call, you all sprint over to the fluorescent flowerpot," Soldier One whispered deeply. "Halt, cat! Abort mission! Abort mission!" exclaimed Soldier One.

"Hush, we need to get back to base, Sergeant!" whispered Soldier Two.

The vicious cat sprang to his feet and heard a bang.

"Shh, the cat's right there!" whispered Soldier One.

Through the miniature peephole in the plant, they could see everything but the cat, with a blink of an eye, they parachuted down the basement.

Robyn Bailey (11)

Harris Primary Academy Chafford Hundred, Chafford Hundred

The Toys' Escape

"Soldiers, stay low, we don't want to make a sound or we'll be eaten," murmured the commander. "Let's move!" he commanded.
The soldiers cautiously crept over the dusty carpet, moving past men that they had lost on their previous attempts. Just then, a boom of a roar shook the ground, it had awoken.
"Run for your lives!" the commander screamed while he and his crew sprinted back as fast as they could. "Hurry, hurry, climb the rope and jump to safety!" boomed the commander.
Finally, they made it up to the windows and jumped out to safety. Another failed attempt!

Benjamin Rumsby (11)

Harris Primary Academy Chafford Hundred, Chafford Hundred

The Lonely Pig

"You're just a loser, Pigglet, go away!" Sam screamed.

Pigglet was the only pig on the windowsill. The only pig holding no money, he was so compact, no one liked or played with him. All of a sudden, he hopped off the windowsill and onto the carpet. He had a plan coming on. He saw some pink paint and decided to pour it over Sam and Ron, *splash!*

"Pigglet, what have you done?" they both yelled.

"I-I don't know, they can't know, the bins will devour us, I'm sorry," Pigglet said.

"It's fine, friends?"

"Friends," they agreed.

Alexi Laken Choppy-Godfrey (10)
Harris Primary Academy Chafford Hundred, Chafford Hundred

Disco Party Fail

The lights switched off. Sophie went to bed. The Barbies jumped out the toy box. *Bang!*
"Oops!" whispered Barbie.
They all made a human ladder so Ken could turn the disco ball on. He pressed the switch and turned the music on. Barbie got into the doll's house and ran to her make-up room and applied her Barbie MAC make-up to get ready for the party.
"Perfect!" said Barbie.
But all of a sudden, Sophie started to wake up.
Ken jumped and turned the light off.
"That was lucky," whispered Ken.
And they all quickly got into the doll's house.

Sophie Hilliard (11)
Harris Primary Academy Chafford Hundred, Chafford Hundred

Toy Jealousy

Dong! Smash! went the delightful vase.
"Quick, everyone hide because Ava's coming!
Move, you scatter-brained robot!"
The robot was Ava's favourite toy whilst all the
other toys were just chucked in the corner.
"Aww! come here you devil robot, I have to go now
but I'll see you tomorrow."
A vicious idea came into the toys' heads.
"Get here ya devoted robot."
All the toys viciously ripped the robot's head off
and took his batteries out. All the toys felt guilty so
they got all the screwdrivers out and fixed it just in
time.

Mia Kaur (11)
Harris Primary Academy Chafford Hundred, Chafford
Hundred

Alien Invasion

This story takes place in a faraway land where toys come to life, nothing is the same and teenage girls can't survive without their cell phones.

"Okay toys, it's time to escape this dusty basement!"

Suddenly, with all their might in the world, the forgotten toys break open the toy box and dash out of the basement, straight to Rachel's room. They turn left and right, forwards and backwards. Rachel is nowhere to be seen.

Suddenly, *bzz, bzz, bzz!* The toys look carefully around the room. Suddenly, they see a vibrating effect. *Bam! Bing!* They are sucked in...

Tatyanna Daisi (10)

Harris Primary Academy Chafford Hundred, Chafford Hundred

The Toy Battle

"Man down, man down!" shouted Commander Robot, trying endlessly to fix his vehicle.
"We're coming!" replied Toe-Town Crew.
The immense sound of power flooded the room between Commander Robot, who was an audacious robot, and the horrible trickster, Officer Bear. He was a mad and uncontrollable bear. He passed Commander Robot arrogantly, after knocking him off course. Commander Robot was back in the race and they were heading for the finish, but a shadow took shape over the course. Everything stopped. A huge foot stomped on the course. The race was over. No one could finish.

Ethan Paul Ridpath (10)
Harris Primary Academy Chafford Hundred, Chafford Hundred

The Enchanted Wood

Charlotte was an unwanted doll that was broken. She dreamt of going to the enchanted wood.

One night, everyone was tucked up in bed beside Charlotte. *This can be the perfect time to escape this place,* she thought. She noticed the window was already open so off she went, walking to her dream place.

As she arrived, she saw glistening fairies singing, elves serving people and parades happening. Charlotte approached this fairy, asking her if she could stay. The fairy said, "Sure," and showed Charlotte her new, cosy home, but first, they joined the parade. This is a beautiful place!

Zoya Ariana Irshad (10)

Harris Primary Academy Chafford Hundred, Chafford Hundred

The Night Creepers

In bed was Isabelle, sleeping.

It was midnight when there was a crash and bang, the lights switched on.

"Finally, we're alone, no sticky hands touching my clothes - urgh! I need to get changed out of this jumpsuit and put some proper make-up on. I look like a clown!"

Barbie ran to the doll's house and put a pink, frilly dress on.

"Oh hi, Ken."

"Hi, let's go, Barbie," shouted Ken.

When they walked out of the doll's house there was a surprise. Isabelle's dog, Lola. She barked and grabbed them with her teeth and put them away.

Isabelle Durant (11)

Harris Primary Academy Chafford Hundred, Chafford Hundred

Saffron's Adventure

There was a puppy, Saffron, who bullied other toys but then Saffron got a lot of attention. The puppy had no friends because of the bullying.

One day the girl, Hailey, got a new toy and she forgot about Saffron.

Ten years later, she was sixteen. She was sorting out her room and came to the toy box then she saw Saffron.

She slowly said, "Saffron!"

But as she yelled that, a girl looked up and said, "Aww!"

Then Hailey knelt down and muttered, "Here you go, keep it safe."

The girl loved Saffron and was so happy and grateful.

Lana Ayeni (10)

Harris Primary Academy Chafford Hundred, Chafford Hundred

The Enemy Of The Lego Bricks

It was a calm, tranquil day. The Lego bricks were up to their normal routine, which was just lying on the carpets and waiting for the humans to play with them. But today, the humans hadn't been to the living room yet. Suddenly, out of nowhere, a human appeared at the door and accidentally stepped onto a Lego brick.

"Oh no!" whimpered one of the Lego bricks!

The Lego bricks stared at the hurt Lego in horror.

"We will have revenge on your humans!" shouted the Lego bricks in anger!

The Lego bricks were madder than ever at humans.

Catherine Tse (11)

Harris Primary Academy Chafford Hundred, Chafford Hundred

The Messy Monkey

As soon as the monkey came alive he saw the handles from the paint bucket. When five minutes went by, he fell. Paint splattered everywhere. Excitedly, behind him, he spotted a brush. The room became a mess. Paint was everywhere.

As ten minutes went by, it became messier. All of a sudden, there was a stomp. *Creak!* went the stairs! A large figure approached.

"Halt!" he said to himself.

The figure wondered why it was a mess. *It must have been the monkey.* She picked the monkey up, threw him out of the window, never to seen again!

Leah Gredley (9)

Harris Primary Academy Chafford Hundred, Chafford Hundred

Happy Moments

Sorrow is like a monster stealing your soul. This was how the forlorn doll was feeling. Her solicitous mother, Carol, was thrown in the abandoned cupboard. Luckily, Carol's child wept tears of despondency. She had a new enemy; the barbarian that stole her precious mother.

Months later, Lucy grew to like this barbarian. Unfortunately, Lucy forgot her mother; her mother didn't forget her. That was all she could think of. One special day, Lucy finally plucked up the intrepidity to save her dear mother. When the two dolls met, not a single eye was dry.

Olaoluwani Ademuyiwa (11)

Harris Primary Academy Chafford Hundred, Chafford Hundred

The Plushies' Adventure

Katie is ten, she loves animals. She has a toy box full of animal plushies, especially cat plushies. Katie left for school. Captain Cheetah assured every plushie the room was safe. They got out of the toy box. Chloe the caracal jumped out the box and ran to Captain Cheetah, being followed by Minnie the cat.

Suddenly, Katie's pet dog started attacking every plushie and ran to the toy box. Unfortunately, Captain Cheetah got bitten by the dog and got taken away. Katie was shocked but luckily, she could sew so she sewed her together and took extra care forever.

Phoebe Sinacola-Webb (10)

Harris Primary Academy Chafford Hundred, Chafford Hundred

Stuffed Animals

I have a secret. Do you promise to keep it? Anyway, I am going to tell you. I have a special diamond that can make my stuffed animals talk. Upsettingly, I had to hide the secret from my parents. Stupidly, I left the diamond next to one of my chattiest teddies. What should I do now?

My mother furiously exclaimed, "If you won't tidy your room, I will need to do it myself!"

I impatiently ran upstairs in devastation.

"Argh!" screamed my mum. "S-s-spider! Chloe, go and get the insect killer!"

Where is the spider...?

Ayobami Oye (10)

Harris Primary Academy Chafford Hundred, Chafford Hundred

The Journey To The Other Room

Barbie missed home, she had to get to Morgan's room. Johnny was asleep, it was time to go. Barbie rode the train to the door. She had never made the journey to the other room on her own. Cautiously, she slipped out of the door. It had never seemed so far! Barbie remembered the carnage that was Johnny's room and it gave her an urge to go faster. "Psst! Psst! Armyboy, here to escort you home," whispered a voice.

It was too late!

Boom! Boom! Johnny came down the corridor, picked up Barbie and some scissors and cut and cut...

Denisia John (11)

Harris Primary Academy Chafford Hundred, Chafford Hundred

A New Home

There were four teddies called Caitlin, Mufaro, Rinnah and Lana. They wanted to leave the home forever but none of the other toys wanted them to leave.

One night, they were thinking what they wanted to do in the morning. Rinnah and Mufaro were going to leave and then come to get us and find a house. In the morning, Caitlin and Lana were trying to distract the rest of the toys. They spotted them!

Bang!

"They saw us!"

Bash! Rinnah grabbed Caitlin and Lana and rushed out of the window, they found a nice, happy home.

Caitlin Emma-Jo Francis (10)

Harris Primary Academy Chafford Hundred, Chafford Hundred

The Lion

The lion was the king of the jungle. His friends are Cheetah, Tiger and Wolf. One day, they were all lying on the grass when the cheetah said, "What's that?"

They pondered, *what if it's dangerous?* But it was too late. *Splat!* A thick red substance came raining down. They were all covered in it.

So the lion said, "I will find out who did this!"

They all went with him. They got to the end of the jungle and nearly fell. They were on a table. They captured a girl.

She said, "You are toys!"

Chloe Harrison (9)

Harris Primary Academy Chafford Hundred, Chafford Hundred

A Birthday Surprise!

One morning, Heaven and Nevaeh woke up with a beaming smile. Heaven pivoted her head towards her dolls and climbed excitedly out of bed and leapt, following the scent of her nose to the kitchen. Nevaeh was already chowing down her pancakes and gulping down her orange juice. As Heaven and Nevaeh were chatting, their mum sneakily grabbed the girls' present to give them. They opened up their present and squealed. Just then, Heaven tripped over her toys and spilt the birthday potion all over their dolls.
Just then, a voice peeped out... "Ouch!"

Rinnah Larbi (10)
Harris Primary Academy Chafford Hundred, Chafford Hundred

Donald's War

"It's clear, all alight positions!" Americans were flanking.

The Brits' body armour prevented them from being shot. Quickly, a giant figure glared over the battle, stopping the fight, *boom!*

"Argh!" Jake the giant woke Hillary and told her that he would help defeat Donald's men.

That's it! Donald woke and they crawled to Hillary's side of the room. *Boom!* "What?" Suddenly, Hillary started waving by but, *slap!* The Americans flew to the other side of the bedroom.

Tayla Shevket (10)

Harris Primary Academy Chafford Hundred, Chafford Hundred

Barbie's Day Out

Barbie woke up from a long nap and went to her dream house closet, picked her outfit and changed from Barbie Night to Barbie Day! Then, she curled her hair and did her make-up.

"Hi, Ken," as she bumped into him.

"Hiya, Barbie."

"Why are you in my house?" she asked, fluttering her eyelashes at him.

"Stacey asked me to fix her muffin maker," said Ken.

"I am gonna go get ready and we can go!"

Everyone stopped.

Paisley awoke and said, "Barbie, what are you doing here?"

Jamie-Leigh Christine Martin (11)

Harris Primary Academy Chafford Hundred, Chafford Hundred

The White Fox

The twilight blanket covered the sky as Monika slept silently; cuddling her favourite plush toy, Arctic, the white fox. The white fox blinked. He blinked again. Slowly, Arctic crept out of his owner's hands. Arctic leapt onto the wooden floor, climbed onto Monika's shelves and stood up gracefully. The fox stepped into a can of ink, making his paws stained black. He steadily pushed off the can. The fox sent a cup of pencils falling down too. All of a sudden, a lamp lit the room. Monika sat up in her bed. She saw Arctic lying on her empty shelves.

Fiona Ng (11)

Harris Primary Academy Chafford Hundred, Chafford Hundred

Tragedy At 12am

Crickets were creaking as the piggy bank was on the lookout for any riches that he was going to face to feed him money. *Clitter clatter, clitter clatter!* went the hooves in the distance. Little Piggy turned around, only to find a teddy bear in a carriage full of coins. He took out his trusty revolver. However, this teddy weren't falling for his dirty tricks. He sprinted towards the pig and smashed him to a million pieces. The teddy bear ran in despair. It woke up. He stared at the floor and wondered how his dear piggy bank had died.

David Gaitan (10)

Harris Primary Academy Chafford Hundred, Chafford Hundred

We Need To Escape!

"Sis, I told you, it's my day with Leo!" demands Jack, the 'elder' bro, there is also a younger sister named Ruby, she is the younger yet more aggressive child.
"Shut your face!"
They have lots of toys and they are absolutely addicted, to be precise, although when they are by themselves they are in a whole different world...
"How dare that disgusting girl grab me," says a lion, "we need to escape, we need to escape."
"I agree, we can do this if we really try!"

Charlie O'Rourke (10)

Harris Primary Academy Chafford Hundred, Chafford Hundred

The Toy Toilet Tragedy

"I need the toilet!" whined Thomas.

"Be fast or we'll miss the bus!" shouted Thomas' mum.

Thomas was a bad boy. He never washed his hands, he never flushed the toilet, all he did was mess around and be revolting. But one thing he loved to do, was play with his toy soldiers all day, all month. Thomas went to the toilet and crammed all his soldiers in his pocket. As he sat on the seat, one fell out and plopped into the water. That soldier drowned and died like a broken ship. He was never seen ever again!

Isabella Gui Susan Rice (9)

Harris Primary Academy Chafford Hundred, Chafford Hundred

Teddy

As the cuddly teddy was sitting on the human's bed, slammed from the human, Teddy said in relief, "I'm free."
Teddy jumped off the bed, wondering what to do. Teddy found a piano carpet lying inside a box in a dusty corner. Teddy was wondering what it was, so Teddy touched it and it made a giant ring. When Teddy slid across the piano, the human heard a loud ring and the human ran upstairs. Teddy heard footsteps approaching the door. The knob slowly turned. Teddy quickly tidied the mess. The door opened...

Carmen May Jones (10)

Harris Primary Academy Chafford Hundred, Chafford Hundred

Toy Trouble

In George's room, there was a toy called Woody and he was George's most favourite toy in the world. George had always played with him. He would use Woody when he played with the soldiers, or when he played car racing with Ferraris. He would never go anywhere without Woody.

Then, one day, Woody had gone missing and could not be found. George was miserable for the rest of the day. Despite that, George still searched for him and would not give up searching. He searched all day and found him under his bed. It was great.

George Sinkins (10)

Harris Primary Academy Chafford Hundred, Chafford Hundred

The War

One day, when Jimmy went to a party, all hundred of his soldiers started shooting Black Panther and Spider-Man. They weren't having any of it, so they started knocking them out and started laughing. All of a sudden, three soldiers came and started punching Black Panther and Spider-Man. So, they kicked the evil soldiers in the bin. The heroes won the battle.

All of a sudden, the door creaked. Everyone hid. Jimmy found them where he hadn't left them so he checked his camera and saw them moving and fighting each other.

Jahziah Blackford (10)

Harris Primary Academy Chafford Hundred, Chafford Hundred

The Robot And The Pig

Once, a robot said to the other toys, "I can do anything."

A shadow loomed over the toys. It dropped something and it left. All the toys ran to the box. Something ripped out of it, it was a pig and a cannon. The new toy got all the attention now. The robot didn't like it.

Robot said, "I'm better than you at shooting out of that cannon!"

The pig said, "Okay, let's see who can go the furthest."

So the pig did it like it was easy. The robot did it. He flew past the pig.

Jamie Broom (10)

Harris Primary Academy Chafford Hundred, Chafford Hundred

Lego

Flying in the sky was a Lego X-Wing battling a Lego TIE Fighter. The fight was leaving Lego all over the floor of the room. Suddenly, the Millennium Falcon got the TIE Fighter down, scattering Lego blocks all around the floor into a minefield of Lego blocks. Just then, the lights turned on. The door opened. The two spaceships crashed into the ground. More Lego scattered. The owner of the Lego stepped forwards then there was a scream of pain.

"Ouch! That hurt!" said the owner of the toys with a red-coloured face.

Evan Williams (11)

Harris Primary Academy Chafford Hundred, Chafford Hundred

Battle Of The Granny And WWE Figures

In an ordinary house with an ordinary boy, there lived Toy, a scary-looking granny doll and some WWE action figures. The granny doll and the action figures were arch-enemies and when they fought the granny, she always won. The figures had a bad leader, James Ellsworth and a bad general, Enzo Amore and then... the figures messed up the leader and general.

The next day, all the figures had a vote. They voted for Roman Reign and Dean Ambrose and when they finally fought Granny, they won. They celebrated happily ever after.

David Nnamchi (10)

Harris Primary Academy Chafford Hundred, Chafford Hundred

The Doll Who Was Alone

There was a doll who lived in a box. She had a white dress that smelt of roses. There was one thing, she was alone. She had no friends and nobody had seen her for twenty years. This was because she lived in a box that had Sellotape all over, there was no way to escape.

One day, she woke up, brushed her hair and got dressed.

An hour later, she heard a noisy van. She looked through her breathing hole. Children were opening the box. Someone took her out and they played happily. She was no longer alone and was happy.

Maria Horsley (9)

Harris Primary Academy Chafford Hundred, Chafford Hundred

The Best Soldiers

One awesome day, an awesome soldier wanted to join the English army, but he couldn't be seen by his buyer. Since they were toys they had to stay still when there were any people around.

One day, the soldier's best friend from school was also going for the spot and they had to be rivals. Just after that, a cat tried to eat them but it was only one of their challenges, so whoever was calm got the point. Then, the next challenge was to fight. The boss told them to stop. They both got the spot. They all cheered!

James Daniel Cooper (10)

Harris Primary Academy Chafford Hundred, Chafford Hundred

Barbie Throughout

Barbie was in her car, racing around when suddenly, the human came. Barbie dropped her lipstick and ran, hiding; then heard the human talking to her mum. She ran out to grab her lipstick then out of nowhere the humans came in through the door. Barbie dropped to the floor then realised she was being lifted by her human and chucked her out of the house. She was one day found by a Barbie lover. But Barbie realised she was never being used, she sat on the shelf all day, every day. The person that admired her was the sister.

Olivia Rose Collard (10)
Harris Primary Academy Chafford Hundred, Chafford Hundred

The Great Escape

A boy named Jack loved playing with his Spitfire. Every day after school, he would play with his toy Spitfire. He would zoom home with satisfaction after every day of school. One day, Jack got back and was fed up with his Spitfire. He threw it on the floor. He always had a dream of becoming an RAF pilot. His life was swell until his dream had broken into three.

Jack had bought a new toy. After school, he realised that his dreams never adjusted but he had changed.

Later on, he became older and gave his son it.

Kelly Ototobor (9)
Harris Primary Academy Chafford Hundred, Chafford Hundred

The Revenge Of The Toys

One day, Kira left for the shops, so the toys came out to play. Once Kira entered the room, the toys hid under the bed. She was holding a new arrival - the new DS.

The next day, when she got back from preschool, she turned the DS on and played for hours.

The toys got cross and planned to break the DS using the army figures. So the next day, they travelled to Jack's room and the army men pushed the DS down. It shattered into millions of pieces. When she got home, she blamed it on her brother.

Elizabeth John (9)

Harris Primary Academy Chafford Hundred, Chafford Hundred

The Beany Boos Run!

The Beany Boos were screwed into a suitcase, so they had to try and escape. Then, they all got out and quickly ran, so someone could play with them. Now they are all running around looking. Then, they saw someone. So they ran even faster, so desperate. They wished they were there already. One of them screamed and shouted, "Yay!"
They could not believe it. Then, when they got there, the girl found them so they got put back by the girl. They were trapped again. They were so disappointed.

Holly Clark (9)

Harris Primary Academy Chafford Hundred, Chafford Hundred

The Last Race

Vroom! The Lamborghini took the lead. The red Ferrari was catching up and it was a tie between the two. What a race that was. It was an incredible one to watch. But they announced there would be another race to declare the winner. "On your marks, get set, go!"

As they raced around the track, the Lamborghini took the lead but the red toy Ferrari caught up. It was neck and neck. It was coming to the end of the race and the Lamborghini won. Oh my god, what a race by the two of them!

Billy Dopson (9)

Harris Primary Academy Chafford Hundred, Chafford Hundred

Toy Stories

One day, a kid played with his World War II planes, he loved them. His mum came into his room, she gave him his iPad. He played with an app called Storm Raiders. He started liking the game until, one night, his toys started moving. They were flying and making noises, it was loud. *Bang, bang, bang! Brrr!* It was like the Battle of Britain.

The next morning, the boy woke up and shouted, "Ouch!"

He trod on his toys. He went to school and he bravely tried not to hurt himself.

Jack Ng (10)

Harris Primary Academy Chafford Hundred, Chafford Hundred

Unicorn And Pegasus

On a lovely, hot summer's day, a little girl named Emma left her house to go to the shops with her mum. Little did she know, her Unicorn and Pegasus toys could walk and talk. They all flew up to the top of her bedroom and then glided back down to the floor.

Emma got home and found her toys scattered across her bedroom floor. The next time Emma went out, she left her tablet on record. When she got home, she watched the video on her tablet and found out that her toys could walk and talk.

Sophie Darrell-Lambert (10)

Harris Primary Academy Chafford Hundred, Chafford Hundred

The Dancing Unicorn

Once, there was a sparkly and glistening unicorn called Tropical Starlight. She loved to dance, she could do hip-hop, ballet and tap but she was forever long dying to learn how to street dance. So she asked one of her unicorn friends, Mackenzie, how to do street dance.

She tried and tried and tried and she was about to give up when Mackenzie said, "Don't be a failure, you can do it!" in a determined voice.

So she tried one more time. She did it and she danced all night.

Nana Nyame (10)

Harris Primary Academy Chafford Hundred, Chafford Hundred

Time To Shine

The door was shut.

"Go, go! Oh sorry, you didn't know the toy could move!"

There would always be a battle with a drone and robot and they would not get along, so they went into battle.

It was their time to shine. The drone could fly but the robot could not fly, the robot could break down, they had a battle.

It was the last person standing, they had to dance for five hours. Who would win it? It was the robot and they became good friends but kept going on.

Sophia Peck (10)

Harris Primary Academy Chafford Hundred, Chafford Hundred

Mr Woof's Great Adventure

In the mist, stood Mr Woof, waiting for his next victim, Tommy. He hid in the darkness then all of a sudden, Tommy came in. Mr Woof pounced into action, bringing Tommy down but Tommy stood back up, throwing Mr Woof off. Then, Tommy woke up and realised it was a dream but he didn't know that lurking the shadows was Mr Woof who was ready to pounce again at Tommy the dreamer, taking him to the floor. But this time with his dog army, Tommy was in for a surprise. What would happen next?

Kevindran Indradas (10)

Harris Primary Academy Chafford Hundred, Chafford Hundred

The Toys

An army of soldiers came over the distance. They planned an escape two years ago and it was ready. They had everything they needed. They started to climb up a wall, the ceiling, to the window. They started to climb down a rope but Jeff, who planned this, fell out the window. They fell down to the ground. They saw a killer clown and picked Jeff up and ran!

Jacob Brown (9)

Harris Primary Academy Chafford Hundred, Chafford Hundred

Secret Life Of Toys

The toys were lonely. The shop was closing down. Once everyone was gone, the toys played. They trashed the place. Then, they all ran away, not just from their box or their shelf. From the shop, for life. A businessman proposed to buy the shop but when he got there, he was appalled and walked straight out and then he cancelled the whole offer.

Naima Muchopa (10)
Harris Primary Academy Chafford Hundred, Chafford Hundred

The Puppet Who Rules!

One day, there was a puppet who did pranks. All his friends were also pranksters. They called themselves 'The Prankers'. They ruled the school but the puppet was better than the rest.
One day, the puppet, Harry, played a prank on the head Stormtrooper. Harry escaped. All of Harry's friends tried to help by throwing pies at the Stormtrooper but the Stormtrooper dodged out the way. When it was just the two of them outside, some army men defended Harry. The head ran away and was never seen again. Harry had won and was voted the coolest puppet in school.

Cadan Robbins (12)

Kingswode Hoe School, Colchester

Robbie's Lost Owner

Once upon a time, there was a robot named Robbie. Robbie was a boy robot, he'd got an owner named Jack.

Jack's mum said, "Jack, we are going to the beach."

Jack took Robbie to the beach.

Fifteen minutes later, they arrived at the beach.

Five minutes later, Jack's mum told Jack to go home, but suddenly, Jack forgot about Robbie! Robbie was sad and lonely so he had a plan. He used his robot eyes to search for Jack. Then suddenly, he found his owner. Robbie used his wheels to get to his owner. Hooray, he'd done it!

Tanya Leonie Norton (12)

Kingswode Hoe School, Colchester

The Story Of The Key Of Destiny

Dolly was a little doll who lived in a dollhouse with her Minecraft wolf, Violet. Dolly had a terrible dream about a master and a key of destiny. Dolly really wanted this special key and went off to get it. The key was kept in a magic castle guarded by Leo and his partner, Zach.

Dolly and Violet climbed the wall and grabbed the key. Leo and Zach chased after them. Dolly climbed onto Violet's back and escaped back to the dollhouse. Violet saved the key.

"Happy birthday, Dolly. I hope you like it," said Violet.

Dolly smiled.

Ellie-May Taylor (12)
Kingswode Hoe School, Colchester

Toxic Destruction

Once upon a time, there was a criminal mastermind, Candy. One day, he decided to make up an evil plan.

"I will meet up with Deathstroke and blow up Ace Chemicals."

The plan was to sneak into Ace Chemicals, past the guards with the electric joy buzzer. Then, they blew up the fuse that controlled the toxic. The toxic made Chocolate City go crazy and shoot out toxic monsters and cannons. Half of the world was covered in toxic. People were starting to burn with fear.

Meanwhile, Candy was on a beach away from it all.

Charlie Evans (12)

Kingswode Hoe School, Colchester

Freddy The Different Bear

One stormy night, in a haunted mansion, there was a boy called Freddy who never interacted with anyone. He lived on his own with just a teddy bear. However, this teddy was different... This teddy came to life! This teddy was so naughty! He jumped house to house and stole people's things to put in his own mansion. The lady across the road saw him stealing so she took a photo and went to the police station. The police went there straight away and the owner and his teddy went to jail.
Now Freddy has no friends at all.

Leanne Wallace (12)
Kingswode Hoe School, Colchester

Dotty's Great Escape

I'm so bored of this toyshop. I want to leave here. Hmm, I have an idea, I could escape at night but what if the owner catches me? I need to think because the owner might lock the door. What if I climb out a window and run. Oh, that might work, yes!

Today is the time I might be able to escape. The owner can't catch me because I can run fast. Yay, I made it! I'm out. Oh, I'm on the streets though.

A friendly boy asks, "Do you need a new home?"

"Sounds great, thank you."

Kian Mills (12)

Kingswode Hoe School, Colchester

Jeff Versus The Sandman

One day Jeff the bear was on the beach exploring with his metal detector. Just then, Jeff heard *bbbbb!* So he dug down and found a handheld Hoover. He carried it along the beach. Suddenly, a Sandman came out of the sand. Jeff felt scared but he knew he could beat the nasty Sandman. Jeff watched the Sandman but then the Sandman made a tornado. Jeff got his Hoover and sucked up the Sandman. Jeff then threw the Hoover so far into the dark, gloomy sea that it was never to be seen again. Jeff celebrated with a swim!

Leo Parsons (11)

Kingswode Hoe School, Colchester

Super Geoff And The Rise Of Gonzo

It was a dark and stormy night. Geoff snuck out of bed. He was so angry at Nigel because he messed up in the rock band. Geoff ran out of the house and into the forest. He didn't know Gonzo was waiting for him. Gonzo disguised himself as an evil music producer and electrocuted Geoff. He tore his disguise apart and he showed his real self. Gonzo fought Geoff and his best friend, Mickey, saved Geoff. Geoff and Nigel made up, got all three pieces of the key and beat Gonzo. They went home and ordered pizzas at home.

Alex Ruske (11)
Kingswode Hoe School, Colchester

Sam And A Lucky Find

There was once a toy soldier called Sam who was hurt in the war. He was sent to the hospital. He saw Doctor Happy. Doctor Happy made Sam feel better with a magic potion of happiness. It healed him and made him smile. Sam wanted to go back to find his army friends. They weren't there. He searched for them and found them in a house. They all searched for the bad guys. They found them and ended the war. They travelled back to camp and met Doctor Happy. The soldiers were all happy and well and had a party.

Lily Eastwood-Bringhurst (11)

Kingswode Hoe School, Colchester

Water Slide Adventure

Once upon a time, there lived a doll, Lisa. She was really little and on holiday in Jamaica. She was on a water slide, it was really fun. Suddenly, there was a spark and she was wiped away to a desert island. She felt so scared and sad, how would she ever be returned to her owner? Katelynn went on the same water slide and guess what? She went to the desert too! She wondered how she was going to get back. Suddenly, she found Lisa and they found a unicorn and a rainbow. The unicorn flew them safely home.

Katelynn Isabella Dixon (11)
Kingswode Hoe School, Colchester

Princess Honey's Party

Princess Honey lived in a palace. Honey was really excited because she was having a party. She was dancing at the party when thieves came in and took the princess through a hole. She felt scared, it was very dark.

At the bottom of the hole, she found a light. She turned it on and saw a bear and monkey running around. The princess asked them where she was. They were shocked to see her but promised to help her. They helped to push her back into the hole and she found her way back to her party.

Kelly Marshall (11)

Kingswode Hoe School, Colchester

Shop To Shop

I'm a Stormtrooper in the wrong toyshop. I must shoot my way through plastic to get back to my shop. I can get onto the tram to get to Miniature Land. I don't know how to get to the tram. I know I must run down the hill to get to it.

I'm off through Miniature Land. I'm halfway to my shop but the sun is rising, I must hurry. I see the tram and I make it. I sneak back into the shop. I'm almost there but wait, ouch! My foot is stuck. Help!

Jay Bass (12)

Kingswode Hoe School, Colchester

All About Me!

One beautiful day, Grumpy was sitting on the beach with her friends. They had brought a picnic with them.

"Can we have the picnic now?" groaned Lazy.

"Yeah, help yourself," answered Jolly.

While everyone was eating, Grumpy wasn't. They were in town by now.

"Can we go to the gym?" asked Mr and Mrs Sporty.

"Fine, if we have to!" moaned Grumpy.

So they went to the gym like they asked. They worked out for an hour! They were so tired after that. They went back to Grumpy's house.

"I'll see you tomorrow then!" yelled Grumpy.

"Yeah, sure."

"Goodnight."

"Bye!"

Ellie Troy-Pryde
St Pius X RC Primary School, Chelmsford

The Rounders Team

Ever since I came to this school, I've dreamed about being on the rounders team. So has my friend Jacob.

"Are you ready to try out for the rounders team?"

"Sure thing!" said Jacob energetically.

After lunch, me and Jacob worked as hard as we could to get the time moving and it worked. It was finally the end of the day.

"Woohoo!" shouted Jacob.

"Quick, let's hurry!" I replied.

We ran and ran and didn't know what time it was.

"You're late!" shouted Coach.

"Sorry Sir, we won't be again."

After that, we got into the rounders team.

"Yay!"

Alanna Ella McDonagh (11)

St Pius X RC Primary School, Chelmsford

Tedious Times

We always are tedious, but ShortySporty never really gets bored. When she does, anything can happen. Let me tell you a time when ShortySporty visited GingerNinja.

It was a clear day and the girls became dreary so they went out on the trampoline.

ShortySporty suggested, "Let's do some flips."

So GingerNinja did a flip and landed on her arm.

There as a deafening crunch!

Her mum came running out and blurted, "You have to go to the hospital!"

When we got there, the nurse explained confidently, "There is an hour wait."

ShortySporty and GingerNinja looked at each other, shocked. "Nooo!"

Maia Dines (10)
St Pius X RC Primary School, Chelmsford

A Short Story About Me!

Tick! Tick! That's the clock. I'm really bored... *Let's watch television!* I thought. When I switched it on, a girl was speaking about herself. Soon... I had a genius idea!

"How about... make a book!" I suggested.

Having decided, I went to my room and started writing. This is how it goes... There once was an altruistic girl named Liethuna (by the way, that's me!). She loved listening to music. She loved reading books. Most of the time, she's on her laptop. She's got many cousins (all older than her). If you've read it, you know a bit about me.

Liethuna Kirikaran (11)
St Pius X RC Primary School, Chelmsford

My Football Team

Last time we played, it ended early because of a storm. Now we have the replay and the crowd is cheering loudly. The whistle blows and the Crawley Cup Final begins!

Before very long, South Iowa are on the attack. They are heading for goal, then suddenly, *whoosh!* The ball explodes before our eyes. Bits are flying everywhere. Someone replaces the ball with a watermelon. What on Earth is going on? Chaos again! However, both teams decide to call it a draw.

The two captains lift the cup and everyone goes off for tea, cake, scones and jam, sandwiches and juice.

Robert Crawley (10)

St Pius X RC Primary School, Chelmsford

The Remote-Controlled Car

"LEGO, we have a car in our lines!" said Officer One.

The car was huge compared to the tiny Lego soldiers. It destroyed the Lego castle then spun around.

"Follow me!" shouted LEGO.

Lego men followed LEGO. The car followed the Lego men.

"Eeek! Stop!" screamed a soldier.

But the car confronted them and forced the men to run back.

"It's better to stay where we are, this car will just follow us!" LEGO said.

The soldiers stopped. The car stopped.

"That's better!" panted LEGO.

"Shhh!" whispered a soldier. "Look!"

Everybody lay still.

"Look!"

"Crash!" shouted Tom.

Kien Tran (8)

The RJ Mitchell Primary School, Hornchurch

The Mystery Forest

A wolf's howl pierced the silence in the night in the deep, dark forest. Surrounded by twisted trees and evil creatures, Rosie and Billy sat clinging onto one another, terrified and scared.

"What was that sound?" asked Rosie.

"There it is again!"

"Oh yeah!" whispered Billy, worryingly. "Maybe it could be a branch, right?"

"What's that in the bushes?" cried Rosie.

"It has glowing yellow eyes and is looking straight at us!"

Suddenly, the fire burnt out and the birds flew away. An owl was tu-whit tu-whooing loudly in the dark forest towards a mystery that would soon arrive...

Chloe Galbraith (8)

The RJ Mitchell Primary School, Hornchurch

Left Behind

"Alex, breakfast is ready!" called Mum.

He jumped up and dropped his toys (Rover the dog, Barnaby Bear and his favourite, Leo the lion) and skidded out the door. Like a click of a switch, they transformed to life.

"Why can't Alex play with us all day?" whimpered Barnaby.

"That's just wrong, he loves us!" exclaimed Rover.

"I've got it! Let's climb into his bag then he'll have to play with us," said Leo. Silently, they crept into the bag. When Alex opened his bag, he was totally puzzled to see his three teddies poking their heads out!

Jasmine Hall (9)

The RJ Mitchell Primary School, Hornchurch

The Great Battle Of The Toys

Flash was having his morning run and saw Reverse Flash. It was already 12pm, three hours after Daniel was in class, which meant it was fight time. The crowd was waiting for them to fight. *Dong! Dong!* The fight had started.

Flash ran straight at Reverse Flash, punching him in the face. There was one hour left before Daniel came home. *Bam! Pow!* Back and forth, they were punching each other like mad, their bodies were hurting, their energy was low, they were tired. Suddenly, Flash threw a lightning strike and ended Reverse Flash's life. Power Flash was very happy!

Daniel Erasmus (8)

The RJ Mitchell Primary School, Hornchurch

Piggy And Evil Octopus

Piggy and Caitlyn both set off to defeat Evil Octopus.

"Come on in!" a dark voice boomed.

Piggy pushed open the door and stepped in. It was very dark and Evil Octopus grabbed them. He threw them in the dungeon and Piggy pulled out a torch. She walked around searching for something that could help them get away. She found a silver key and rushed over to the cell door but before she got there, the torch's batteries ran out. She used her hands and found the keyhole.

"Come on!" Piggy shouted.

They ran out of the castle holding hands.

Lily Cain (9)
The RJ Mitchell Primary School, Hornchurch

The Teddy Bear Picnic

The teddy family were packing up their picnic. They got to the front door, Jam opened the door then everyone started running to the middle of the field. The grass looked green and birds looked pretty. They put the wooden picnic basket down.

Jam mumbled and said, "Do you know what the weather is?"

Toffee screamed, "No!"

Next, Doughnut saw the picnic floating in the air. One hour later, pancakes started falling down from the sky. Next, butter rained down from the sky. It started getting heavy so everyone started running back home.

Nicole Martine (8)

The RJ Mitchell Primary School, Hornchurch

The Dinosaur Who Lost His Teddy

Sixty-five million years ago, there was a dinosaur called Rory who roamed the forest during the Cretaceous period. Rory was a hungry male dinosaur who loved to eat meat.

One day, while out hunting, he lost his favourite teddy called Tim. Rory looked everywhere! Even up the tallest tree in the forest. Although, on the way down, he lost his grip and went falling down as fast as a lightning bolt. But then, he noticed a little teddy bear ear poking out of his bed. It was Tim. "Yippee! I have been looking for you!" said a very happy Rory.

Harrison Cotton (9)

The RJ Mitchell Primary School, Hornchurch

The Evil Bear And The Unicorns

Despite the fact that it was windy, it was a glamorous day. Nikki the unicorn wanted to go for a peaceful picnic in the woods. It was lovely in the woods. Nikki walked deeper and deeper into the forest. Suddenly, a purple bear jumped out and grabbed her! The evil bear took her to his trash bin lair. Nikki was really scared and she hoped someone would save her. The evil bear wanted to have unicorn soup.

Then suddenly, out of the blue, a handsome, young unicorn prince came to her rescue and he stabbed the very, very wild bear.

Ara Kayode (8)

The RJ Mitchell Primary School, Hornchurch

Driver Of A Train

My heart was pounding. The bridge in front of me had broken, snapped to pieces. I tried to push the brake as hard as I could with my hand until it hurt. My only thought was the 146 passengers on board, I was responsible for them. I felt panicky, sweaty and slightly dizzy. We were now slipping and slipping and slipping across the railway. There was no hope. Thinking, *I'm too young to die.*
"Bobby, teatime," called Mum.
I felt relief, I gasped with joy. It was just my imagination.

Bobby Alan Wakeling (9)
The RJ Mitchell Primary School, Hornchurch

Stack

"Yellow, we're on Plan Y!" shouted Red Brick.

"Everybody, stack!" ordered Yellow.

Every brick in the bedroom listened dutifully and started to stack.

"We're almost there!" voices yelled encouragingly.

"Drop down!" Black cried, hearing footsteps thundering up the stairs.

The doorknob turned. They hid in fear. In came Ava, the evil owner's sister. "Come on, bricks," Ava whispered, "let's go."

Could it be true? Ava had come to save them. They'd heard the rumours. Ava's bedroom was a peaceful and happy place where toys were treated with affection and respect. They couldn't believe their luck.

"Mission accomplished!" said Red, winking.

Caleb Mills (9)

Wells Primary School, Barclay Oval

The Unexpected Rescue

"What an adventure!" cried Josie Bear. "I can't wait to tell Mum what happened!"

"How are we getting out of Annabelle's bedroom?" asked Fluffy Bunny.

"The return device is in the bag. Quick! Fluffy, Josie, hop in!" exclaimed Rainbow Unicorn.

Frowning suddenly overcmae her face.

"It's broken! We can't get home now!"

"I've got decent maps, but it'll be an arduous walk," suggested Josie.

"Will a helicopter come and save us, perhaps?" questioned Fluffy.

"In this cold weather... no way!" sighed Rainbow. "We'll just have to go the long way."

Then, to everyone's surprise, a helicopter came to rescue them!

Sophia Tse (9)

Wells Primary School, Barclay Oval

The Great Mission

"You stay and look out, John," commanded Infinity, "and Stretchman, you and I will go downstairs." Infinity rapidly darted while Stretchman took it slow, as if he was on a tripwire.

"Incoming!" cried John. "There is their car!"

"Quick, come on, Stretchman! Up we go!"

Infinity and Stretchman pulsed up the stairs. Phew! Infinity and Stretchman had just made it before Anthony's mum opened the door. Anthony climbed up the wooden stairs.

"Nope, no damage," he told himself.

"Mission complete!" whispered Infinity, as Anthony left the room as the light went off.

The toys had made it.

Benjamin Samuel Bennett (9)
Wells Primary School, Barclay Oval

A New World

There once lived, on a planet called Ijome, bright beaming emojis. Life was blissful until one mysterious morning when everything changed. The air turned cold. Frantic, callous aliens rampaged them. The planet cracked open like an egg. Thankfully, Crier, an emoji, escaped. Propelled into orbit, he crash-landed onto Earth with an "Argh!" Yellow sunflowers surrounded him. He rolled himself out of the field. There, he met a golden-haired boy.

"I'm Jim," he said.

Crier cried, "My planet's been destroyed!"

Jim had a plan.

He scanned Crier into his phone, created a new Ijome, saying, "Be brave. Never cry again!"

Austin MacDonald (9)
Wells Primary School, Barclay Oval

Anything Can Happen!

I slammed my bedroom door; its thunderous crash reverberated through my room.

"What a terrible day!"

A solitary tear trickled over my gloomy cheeks.

"We need to help her..."

I turned to find the gentle, hazel eyes of my favourite bedtime tiger observing me.

"Huh?" was all I could mutter in disbelief. "How?"

My menagerie of soft toys had crept towards me and I was confronted by a velvety, chattering zoo of a camel, tiger, turtle and bear.

"You're surprised we can talk? If you believe in yourself, anything is possible," came the reply that transformed my horrible, sad day.

Lani Oshungbure (9)

Wells Primary School, Barclay Oval

Pokémon Adventure 2

When I woke up on Friday, it was my birthday. All I was thinking about was toys. All I got were Pokémon toys...

"Oi, Pikachu?"

"Yes, commander?"

"Why don't you do thunderbolt attack and I will do a flame roar?"

"Bulbasaur, throw some lives!"

"Bulbasaur, why are you being so quiet?"

"Pikachu, Charmander, that's because I am concentrating on my moves, that is why I am so quiet."

"Bulbasaur, I thought you already knew your moves. Quick, hide, the boy is coming. Hide under the big bed. Oh, I can't believe it is Mega Mewtwo, he is here!"

Lynden Kyte (9)

Wells Primary School, Barclay Oval

What A Picnic!

"What a wonderful day!" sighed Mariana.

All of her brown teddies were sitting around a picnic blanket with biscuits. Mariana was having a delightful picnic with her furry friends, all sitting in a shady spot! *Drip, drip, drip!* It was starting to rain. Mariana snatched her petticoat and her plate and vanished inside.

"Oh! My clothes!" cried Mimi, a doll.

"We must do something!" cried Soldier.

"I know," cried Jimmy, an old, tatty teddy. He explained his genius plan.

Then, all the toys made a clothes chain, hurled it towards Guy's window. He grabbed the rope and they scrambled up!

Emily Flora Bell (9)

Wells Primary School, Barclay Oval

98

A Very Bad Day!

As a gleeful boy called Andy woke up, his sly and sneaky plushies had just finished planning their positions.

"Alright, Jeffy, you're in charge of distracting Andy whilst Bob is in charge of lookout," commanded Fred, the Red.

"Hey, what about my precious job?" questioned Squidward.

"Sorry bud, you don't have one," explained Fred the Red with a voice quite gentle.

Speechless, Squidward darted into the corner of the humongous bed. Fred now felt really guilty, so he strode over to cheer him up. Unfortunately, Squidward died because when Fred came over, there was too much weight in the corner.

Viktor Zaykov (9)
Wells Primary School, Barclay Oval

The Secret Life Of Toys

"I think it's clear," whispered Nerf Gun.

"Thank you," replied the robot, "looks like all systems go!"

All the toys in Tony's bedroom woke up as Tony fell asleep. This meant it's party time! The robot started to get a bit mad. He started a magic show that everyone loved and they all sat and watched him do the same tricks repeatedly. "Grunt!" the robot screeched.

Tony awoke and had seen what his toys had been doing.

"My toys are real!" Tony exclaimed. "That's why my room has been a mess lately!"

Now they had some serious talking to do!

Sahib Panjrath (9)

Wells Primary School, Barclay Oval

Eli's Catastrophe

Eli sat on the bed anticipating Millie picking her up.
Millie walked straight past! Eli's heart dropped. She
felt confused. Why? Did Millie have a new favourite
toy? What would happen to her? She was afraid.
She had heard about the loft, the place where toys
disappear forever. Eli was terrified. She shook and
shivered, her heart pounded.
The loft was dark and creepy. The loft had spiders.
She wanted to run but was frozen to the spot.
Tears rolled down her cheeks. What would become
of her? Suddenly, she was high in the air in Millie's
arms, safe again.

Millie Ryan-Martin (7)
Wells Primary School, Barclay Oval

The Lost Wand

In a toy store, no one knew where a toy witch called Genty lived. Her face was grey and she had wrinkles like a crumpled-up, old tissue.

Jack the toy prince was such a show-off and very mischevious. One day, he quietly crept into her room and swapped her wand with a worm.

Genty asked everyone, "Have you seen my wand?"

Genty was furious when she saw Jack turning everyone into frogs. He was so occupied, he didn't notice Genty creeping up behind. She banished him through a Lego portal forever. She turned all of the toys back to normal.

Amar Johal (8)

Wells Primary School, Barclay Oval

There Is No Such Thing As Girls' And Boys' Toys!

I wish I could travel the world and visit Boys' Toy Land... I'm Ellie, a unicorn squishy and I live in Girls' Toy Land. We aren't allowed in Boys' Toy Land and I want to change that. My secret plan was to find Harry, a celebrity squishy who I loved. A fluffy cloud dropped me at Harry's grand mansion and we agreed my plan! We made a convincing speech to everyone, explaining the way girls' and boys' toys should play together.

Amazingly, Harry had fallen in love with me and we ended up living happily with all different toys!

Sofiina Jones (9)

Wells Primary School, Barclay Oval

Far Away From Home

Hi, I'm Pipsqueak, Reggie's cuddly toy meerkat. I was originally from London Zoo but I was adopted by a kind boy called Reggie. I live with him and all his other toys.

One day, I had a dream about home and my caring family. I realised how much I missed them and wanted to see them again. That evening, I decided it was time! I sneakily crept out of the house and scampered through the stinky sewers until I reached London Zoo. I heard familiar noises and there, lurking in the dark, was my family.

"Come home, Pipsqueak!" they cheered.

Reggie Oliver-Simmons (8)
Wells Primary School, Barclay Oval

Maisy's Little Life

As the sun rose on the cold, misty morning, Maisy (the toy bird) looked out of the window. As soon as the heavy door closed and her little girl went to school... she knew she was doomed. Although the kittens were extremely cute, Maisy knew they were vicious hunters. Even though she was scared, she was very intelligent. The cats began to glide upstairs stealthily. The door creaked and they were ready for a showdown. Quickly, the cats pounced and Maisy fluttered, her wings sparkled in the sunlight. Had she escaped their deadly, evil clutches?

Bella Hall (7)

Wells Primary School, Barclay Oval

Computer Magic

One lovely, sunny day, Lola was sitting in front of her computer playing Roblox. Then, all of a sudden, her face got stuck onto the computer screen. She tried to unstick her face from the computer but she couldn't. Then, the computer sucked her in one gulp. She realised she was made out of cubes and all other kinds of shapes! She ran to the front of the computer screen and started hitting it so somebody could hear her. She even started screaming for help but nothing could be done to save her. She was locked in the world of games.

Yoanna Peteva (9)
Wells Primary School, Barclay Oval

Pokémon Adventure

There was a happy city, Ninjago. In there was a ninja called Kai and his friend called Lucrio and Pikachu. One day, in the sky, there was a purple hole. Suddenly, Mewtwo froze the city.

Two weeks later, people were thrown out of the city. They took their things down. Everyone split and went somewhere else. Kai and his friends tried to make a plan to defeat. Then, Kai said the crystal could defeat it. They went to Ninjago City and threw the crystal to Mewtwo and came back to Ninjago City and the master, Kai, had a great party.

Kayra Demir (9)
Wells Primary School, Barclay Oval

Teddy's First Hug

"Where am I?" All I could see were toys. They told me I was in a toyshop.

"Hello!" a loud voice was shouting at me.

I was so shocked my heart missed a beat. It was a little girl staring at me. Her smile made me happy. *Whack! Bang! Whoosh!* When I opened my eyes, it was pitch-black and on top of me was strange paper. Suddenly, someone was tearing it open and pulling me out to freedom. The girl with the beautiful smile was hugging me.

It was my first bear hug ever. I felt lucky!

Kyra Mubashar (7)
Wells Primary School, Barclay Oval

The Hand And The Three Toys

Once upon a very weird and wonderful time, there were three toys which were always fooling around on the computer when no one was looking. They were always taking fantastical but also crazy pictures of themselves, like one when they were next to the picture frame of the girl (she was the owner of those toys, even though she was thirteen years old).

One very quiet and peculiar night, when everyone went to sleep, the toys as always, were playing on the computer, but then a red and black hand appeared. It took them!

Adeeba Khandokar (9)
Wells Primary School, Barclay Oval

Dog Disaster!

One glorious day, I was happily playing in my colourful, huge garden with my cute, brown toy dogs. There were four adorable dogs called Luke, Chewy, Flossy and Lola. They were all tiny jug puppies. Just as I decided to put them on their long, multicoloured leads, they turned into real dogs! I couldn't believe my eyes, I was so shocked because it was my dream come true. I was really happy but worried because, what if my parents saw? Oh no, they were coming, what should I do? Help!

Mirabelle Rose Morgan (9)

Wells Primary School, Barclay Oval

Est.1991

YOUNG WRITERS INFORMATION

We hope you have enjoyed reading this book – and that you will continue to in the coming years.

If you're a young writer who enjoys reading and creative writing, or the parent of an enthusiastic poet or story writer, do visit our website **www.youngwriters.co.uk**. Here you will find free competitions, workshops and games, as well as recommended reads, a poetry glossary and our blog.

If you would like to order further copies of this book, or any of our other titles, then please give us a call or visit **www.youngwriters.co.uk**.

Young Writers
Remus House
Coltsfoot Drive
Peterborough
PE2 9BF
(01733) 890066 / 898110
info@youngwriters.co.uk

 @YoungWritersUK    @YoungWritersCW